Why Doesn't She Go Home!

Why Doesn't She Go Home!

by Bonnie Towne

Cover illustration by
Bill Robison

Published by Willowisp Press®, Inc.
401 E. Wilson Bridge Road, Worthington, Ohio 43085

Printed in the United States of America

10 9 8 7 6 5 4 3 2 1

ISBN 0-87406-119-9

To Mindy and Alyn

One

IN the first place I was mad because we had to get up at 6:30 in the morning to drive to the airport to pick up my cousin Jennifer. In the second place I was mad because we had to miss swim practice to go get my dumb cousin. So when she came down the escalator looking like a model in those magazines that Mom buys, I was in no mood to put up with her garbage.

"Aunt Liz!" Jennifer called, waving. How embarrassing! She looked gross. She was wearing a wild pink outfit you could see a mile away. Besides that she wore shiny eye shadow and lipstick.

Jennifer is only a year and a half older than I am. That's too young for all that gook. After all, she's only thirteen.

"So good to see you," she gushed. She was hugging Mom. "And how are you, Laurie? Hi, David." She squeezed my hand even though I didn't offer it.

"Oh, fine." I tried to smile.

David was grinning at her like an idiot. He does that to Robin Kinzler at school who has big you-know-whats. "Hi, Jennifer," my twin brother said. "We're glad you came."

"My, David, how grown up you are for only eleven years old," Jennifer said in that syrupy voice. She pushed her blonde hair back on her forehead and batted her long eyelashes at him.

"We're so glad to see you," Mom said, taking her arm. They started walking to the baggage claim area. "Did you have a good flight, Jennifer?" Mom asked.

David walked on the other side of Miss Celebrity, so there was nothing for me to do but tag along behind. That was fine with me. I wouldn't want anyone to think I was with that funny-looking creature.

"Yes, it was a wonderful flight. There was a college boy in front of me who kept trying to talk to me."

Oh, brother, I thought. She's boy-crazy, too.

"How's your family, Jennifer?" My mother asked, changing the subject.

That was the wrong question, because Jennifer launched into a twenty-minute discussion about the relatives I don't even know. How boring.

It took a half hour to locate all four pieces of Jennifer's sky blue luggage. She's only going to be here for two weeks, I thought. Then Jennifer wasted some more time moaning and groaning over every little scratch on her new luggage.

When we finally got back home, it was lunchtime.

"Laurie, why don't you show Jennifer where she'll be sleeping and help her unpack her things. I'll fix some sandwiches for lunch," Mom said.

"Oh, I don't eat bread," Jennifer said. "I'm on a diet." She wiggled her hips. She didn't look like she needed to be on a diet to me.

Mom put her lips in a straight line like she does before she gets mad at David or me. "Well, what would you like for lunch, Jennifer?"

"Aunt Liz, would it be too terribly much trouble to make a little salad?" Jennifer batted her eyes.

"It would be no trouble at all." Mom opened the refrigerator. "You girls go unpack while I get lunch ready."

When I went to camp last summer, I unpacked in ten minutes, but not Jennifer. Not only did she have to refold every pair of underpants, but she had to hang up all her shirts and pants as well.

"Only one drawer for me?" she asked, as she arranged her shorts, tops, underwear, and pajamas in the drawer I had cleared out for her. "Where can I keep my makeup?"

"I don't know. The others are full." I looked in the drawers.

"Maybe I can use the bathroom," she said. Then she marched into the bathroom I shared with David and began removing all the washcloths from the drawer. Soon she had the drawer filled with enough cosmetics to start her own drugstore.

I walked out to the kitchen where David was waiting for lunch. "It's going to be a long two weeks," I said.

"Don't worry, Sis. It'll get better once Jennifer gets used to us," David said. "Just because she's a New Yorker is no reason to panic."

"I don't know." I remembered the drugstore of cosmetics in the bathroom drawer.

Jennifer walked into the kitchen. She had put on more lipstick, and she had brushed her hair. She had a blue ribbon wrapped around all that blonde hair. She did look kind of neat for a minute, I thought.

"You kids can go to the lake this afternoon," Mom said.

I gave her a poison look. "But Mom, I want to go to late swim practice since I missed the morning one."

"I'll go," David volunteered. He sat on the stool next to Jennifer, never taking his eyes off her.

"It won't hurt you to miss practice for one day," Mom said, giving me her "or-else" look.

"I can't go to the lake until I go shopping for a new bathing suit," Jennifer said. "My last year's suit is too kiddish, if you know what I mean." She stuck out her chest leaving no doubt about what she meant. "Mother gave me money to buy a new suit. Do you think we could go shopping first?" she asked.

I took a big bite of my peanut-butter sandwich and chewed hard. I hate shopping. Mom usually only makes me go once a year before school starts. The rest of the time she buys things my size and brings them home.

Mom looked at her watch. "Well, I guess we could go." Mom isn't the world's greatest shopper either.

"You don't want to go shopping do you, David?" I asked.

"I wouldn't miss it for the world." David grinned.

So off we went to the mall. Jennifer got excited when she saw the long row of stores. "Oh, good," she exclaimed. "There are lots of stores to choose from."

Mom looked at me, and I looked at her. But we didn't say anything. I'd had a feeling this day was trouble from the start.

We went to a department store first. Mom figured they'd have the biggest selection in the mall.

"It's so hard to buy a bathing suit," Jennifer said as she browsed through rack after rack. "You just never know what it's going to look like on."

"What color are you looking for?" I asked.

"Whatever looks the best," she said. Jennifer smiled mysteriously. "Except for green, of course. . .I hate green."

"There are some more suits over here," I said, crossing to another rack. "I'll look through these."

Mom had found a chair near the mirror. David was leaning against the wall, ogling Jennifer.

I found a pink suit with black polka dots and ruffles. Somehow it reminded me of Jennifer. "What do you think of this one?" I asked, taking it over to her.

"Well, it might do," she answered, holding it up. "We'll see how it looks." She added the suit to the group she had collected.

"May I help you with those?" a saleslady asked. She took the huge pile of suits and hangers from Jennifer. "Would you like to try these on?"

"Yes," Jennifer said. "But I want to finish looking first. I wouldn't want to miss anything."

"You can only take three suits into the dressing room at a time," the saleslady said.

"That's all right. My cousin will hand them to me," Jennifer told the lady.

I rolled my eyes at Mom. She shrugged. What could we do? We were stuck with Miss Finicky until she decided to buy a bathing suit.

David stared at Jennifer a while longer. Then he wandered off to the TV and stereo department.

Jennifer finally decided to start trying on the mountain of swimsuits. I wished for once I were with David.

Jennifer tried on all the suits, and NOTHING satisfied her. "It's too tight across the chest." "The color does nothing for me." "It's too long in the body." "It's too short in the body." She had a million excuses why the suits wouldn't do. And I had to listen to every one of them.

"Maybe we should try another store," I suggested when Jennifer had rejected the last one.

Jennifer's face brightened. "Oh, yes, let's. I can try on lots more."

I knew I had made a mistake. I pictured us growing old and gray, with Jennifer still trying on swimsuits.

When we emerged from the dressing room, David was standing with Mom. "Did you find one?" he asked Jennifer.

"No, we're going to try another store," Jennifer said.

David's mouth dropped open, and he rolled his eyes. He couldn't believe what a big production this was either.

So we spent the whole afternoon shopping at the mall. Jennifer tried on a zillion bathing suits and strutted in front of every mirror in every store in the mall.

Toward the end, Mom looked at her watch

and grumbled under her breath a lot. "We'll have to find something soon, Jennifer," she said. "I need to get home to start dinner."

Jennifer didn't get the message. She kept on looking for the perfect bathing suit.

Mom sat in a chair in the last store. Her lips made a hard thin line. Jennifer came prancing out in a slinky pastel one-piece with diagonal stripes. It made her pale skin look even paler.

"That looks fine, dear," Mom said. "Don't you think so, Laurie?"

"Yeah, it looks great," I lied.

"It does look great," David said. I thought he was sick or something.

"I'll take it," Jennifer said slowly. I looked hopefully at Mom. "The New York stores have a better selection," Jennifer said. "But I'll take it." Mom frowned at me.

"Fine." Mom snatched the ticket off the suit and hurried to the checkout counter.

* * * * *

It was nearly five when we finally arrived at the lake. We found a spot on the beach and spread out our towels.

"Let's go swimming first and then lay in the sun," I suggested.

"Oh, no," Jennifer said. "I don't want to get my new suit wet—it might fade. You go ahead. I'll work on my tan." She rubbed tons of that sickening sweet-smelling suntan oil on her white skin.

I went in swimming. I couldn't stand to breathe that stuff any longer. I tried to practice my strokes, but it wasn't like swimming in the pool. A whole day wasted! I thought.

I got out of the water and collapsed on the towel beside Miss Beauty Queen. "Why did you buy a suit if you're not going to swim?" I asked.

"To get a tan, of course," she answered.

"I'm on the swim team, you know. I won two first place ribbons in the last meet."

"How nice," she said.

"Maybe you'd like to watch me swim in the next meet."

"Perhaps. But I'm not very interested in swimming."

"How come?" I asked.

"I don't swim."

"You mean you don't know how?"

"I never bothered to learn," she said. Then she rolled over onto her stomach. "Is that your swim team suit?"

"Yes." I smiled.

"I figured it must be. No one would buy a shapeless thing like that just to wear."

I dug my toes hard into the sand. Boy, was it going to be a long two weeks.

Two

THE problem with my cousin staying with us was that she had to go everywhere I went. Like when we went to the swim meet in Forest Bay, Jennifer had to tag along. If she hadn't gone with us, she wouldn't have met Bernie Wysowski. That was the point where my life really got complicated.

Bernie Wysowski isn't any ordinary kid. He happens to be the captain of the swim team, the best swimmer on the team, and the most handsome boy I've ever seen in my life. He and David are best friends even though he is two years older than we are. Sometimes he even comes over to our house which is fun for me, because I have secretly liked him since fourth grade. But I haven't told anyone, not even David.

Anyway, Jennifer waltzed out in a bright purple jumpsuit with no straps that made me suck in my breath when I saw her. I tried to get Mom to make her change before we went to the meet. But she wouldn't do it.

When we got to the pool, everybody stared at Jennifer. You would have thought she was a movie star. David went right over to Bernie, and I could see them talking about Jennifer and giving her the once over.

"All swimmers who need a ride line up over here," Coach Bob Ashley announced.

A line of kids formed next to the coach. Bob matched up parents who were driving with swimmers who needed a ride. I heard David say, "We'll take Bernie with us."

That's when all the trouble began. Jennifer, the big sneak that she is, didn't sit in the back with David and Bernie. That would have been too obvious. She sat in front with me and spent the whole trip turning around and flirting with Bernie.

"Tell me about swimming," she said. "I've never been to a swim meet before."

"There are four strokes, see?" Bernie began.

Jennifer's perfume was making me sick. I had this empty feeling in my stomach, and I couldn't breathe. No matter what she said, Bernie and David laughed and teased her back. Bernie had never talked that way with me.

"Laurie, explain to Jennifer what a flip turn is," David said.

"Why don't you tell her yourself? You seem to be doing all the talking," I snapped. Jennifer just looked at me.

"You'll have to forgive my sister," David said. "She gets a little uptight before meets."

"Speak for yourself, David," I said. "I just don't happen to think you're very funny that's all."

There was a moment's pause, and then they went on talking as if I had never said anything. They didn't address any more questions to me though. I guess you aren't with it unless you can flirt like my cousin.

When we got to the Forest Bay pool, I got away from Jennifer as fast as I could. I stood with the other eleven- and twelve-year-old girls on the swim team.

"Who's that girl that rode with you?" Melissa Jones wrinkled up her nose. She always wrinkles up her nose at everything except the things she approves of, which aren't very many.

21

"That's my cousin, Jennifer. She's visiting us for two weeks." I noticed Jennifer was still surrounded by David, Bernie, and the other boys.

"She's so white," Melissa said in her whiney voice.

"She's from New York and doesn't get out much," I said.

My stomach still ached at the way Bernie smiled at her.

"Where's Gail Fortis?" asked Allyson Bradley, the best eleven-year-old swimmer.

"She has a sore throat," I said.

"Then you'll get to swim in the relay," Susie Wheeler whispered. Susie always whispered everything as if it were a big secret.

Normally I would be all excited about swimming in the relay, but all I could do was watch Jennifer and the boys. I couldn't even get the ache in my stomach to go away when I stood on the starting block to swim the freestyle in the relay.

My dive was short, but I stayed even with the Forest Bay freestyler until the turn. The other girl's turn was perfect. It put her one length ahead of me.

"Come on, Laurie!" Coach Bob yelled.

"Pull! Pull!" everybody screamed.

I pulled as hard as I could. I got extra power from somewhere, but it wasn't enough. The Forest Bay team won by one stroke.

The home team cheered loudly. I climbed out of the pool, panting. Allyson, Susie, and Melissa were waiting for me, disappointment on their faces.

"Why didn't you pull?" Melissa whined.

"I did," I told her. A lump rose in my throat. One by one the tears started to slide down my face, and I couldn't stop them. I felt like such a jerk. Jennifer was sitting there with a smirk on her face. Bernie and David were watching me, too.

"You did your best. And you almost beat them," Allyson said.

Coach Bob came over and put his arm around me.

"I lost it for them," I said to him.

"Hey, you have it all wrong," he said. "You didn't lose it. The other team just barely won it. You didn't swim badly, Laurie. The other team just swam better."

Coach Bob walked me back to the benches. My face was hot, and I longed to dive into the pool and never come up. This was the first time I'd had a chance to swim in a relay, and I had botched it.

Later when I was no longer the center of attention, David came over. "Hey, Sis, cool it, okay? If you lose a race, so what? Nobody is going to behead you."

I knew he was just trying to make me feel better. But when I looked at him, I didn't see my brother who was the closest person to me in all the world. I saw Jennifer's admirer, one of the enemy. I felt betrayed.

"Forget it, David. I can take care of myself," I said.

He looked surprised and hurt. I turned away from him and pretended to watch the meet. I felt like crying more than ever now. David gave up and walked back to the other boys. I began to hate Jennifer so much. Since she had come here, nothing had gone right. Now she had turned my own brother against me.

*　*　*　*　*

When we were getting ready for bed later that night, Jennifer said, "You sure get upset when you don't win the race, don't you?"

"I don't see where that's any of your business," I told her.

"New Yorkers would never get so uptight about an athletic event. We have too many other things to do," she said.

"Don't preach at me, Miss Perfect. You come here from New York and think you know everything. Well, you don't. So lay off." I turned out the light and plopped on the bed.

"You don't have to get huffy about it," she said.

I gritted my teeth to keep from fighting with her some more. I reminded myself how glad I would be when her two weeks were up.

Three

WHEN David, Gail Fortis, and I got to morning practice, the floating plastic-covered ropes that divided the pool into six swimming lanes were already in place. Susie came running up when she saw us.

"Want to play water polo?"

"I want Gail on my team," said Bernie, the other team captain.

"I said it first," Susie said.

"But you said Laurie, not Gail," Bernie answered. "You take Laurie and David. I'll take Gail."

"I will not. I said it first," Susie said again.

The argument ended when Bernie fell into the pool, knocking Susie in with him. They thrashed around in the shallow water, grinning and shrieking at each other. Everybody laughed except me. It wasn't exactly fun to have them fighting over *not* having me on their water polo team. Gail makes me sick. She swims fast and is good at all sports.

The shrill tweet of Coach Bob's whistle put an end to the noise. "Save your energy. You're going to need it."

"Oh, no," Melissa whined. "He means fifty laps again today."

"That's right." Coach Bob grinned. "Eight and unders in lane one. Ten and unders in lane two. You know the rest. Get going."

"We swim in lane three, right, Susie?" I ran to catch up with her.

"Yeah," Susie whispered. "Did you know that Melissa and Gail didn't swim their laps yesterday? They only swam forty and lied about the rest."

"I wondered how they finished so long before I did." We reached the rest of the girls and didn't say any more. We both knew we would never cheat at practice. Swimming the length of the pool fifty times is tough, but it makes us better swimmers.

I was swimming along, concentrating on my strokes, when Gail swam up beside me in the lane.

"Do you mind if I pass you?" she asked.

"You're slowing me up."

"Mind? Why should I mind?" I asked.

Gail grinned and swam around me. She cheats by not swimming her laps, I thought. And she still swims faster than me. Sometimes I wonder why I bother to work so hard.

* * * * *

"I had a letter from Aunt Karen today," Mom said when we got home from swim practice. Jennifer was outside working on her tan.

"Did she say when Jennifer is leaving?" I asked.

"Be quiet," David said. "Let her finish."

"Sometimes when people are married a while, they change so much that they become incompatible. Do you understand that?"

"I think so," I said.

"You mean they can't live together without fighting," David said.

"Yes. Aunt Karen and Uncle Hugh are getting a divorce," Mom told us. "Of course, they both still love Jennifer very much, but they don't want to stay married."

"Gosh," I said.

"Poor Jennifer. Will she still live in the

same house?" David asked.

"That's what I wanted to talk to you about. Aunt Karen asked if Jennifer could spend the rest of the summer with us while she finds an apartment and a job."

"The rest of the summer with us?" I echoed with surprise. "No way am I going to put up with Miss Stuck-up for three months. After all, I'm the one who has to give up half of my room and most of my closet." Also my brother and Bernie Wysowski, I thought, but I didn't say it aloud.

"Laurie, we just can't say 'no' to your Aunt Karen."

"But Mom, you know how Jennifer is. She drives me up the wall. I'm positive I can't take a whole summer of her." I stood up and raised my voice hoping Mom would realize that I meant business. My stomach began to hurt.

"Does Jennifer know yet?" David asked.

"No, I wanted to talk to you and Laurie first," Mom said.

"She doesn't spend any time with us anyway," I snapped. "All she does is flirt with boys."

"Laurie, calm down," David said. "I can't understand why Jennifer bugs you so much. She has to stay the summer, and that's that.

You might as well make the best of it."

"That's easy for you to say," I yelled at him. "You don't have to share your room with her."

I could have killed David for putting on his I'm-more-reasonable-than-you act. I should have known better than to count on him for support where Jennifer's concerned.

"Laurie, please," Mom said. "I think you're being selfish."

"But, Mom . . . I'm being honest. Why don't you write Aunt Karen. Tell her we're sorry about the divorce and everything, but we can't possibly keep Jennifer." I knew I was losing ground, but I didn't know how to stop it. David stared at me like I had three heads or purple eyes or something.

The thought of Jennifer around all summer made me sick. Pictures of Bernie and Jennifer laughing and holding hands popped into my head.

Jennifer walked in the front door. "What's going on?"

"We're just talking," David said.

"Jennifer, I had a letter from your mother today," Mom told her.

"Oh, good. What did she say?"

"Well, your mother wants you to stay with us for the rest of the summer."

"She does? Why?"

"Jennifer, you know your parents have had problems getting along. Sometimes it's better for a couple not to stay together if they aren't happy." Mom put her arm around my cousin. "Honey, I'm sorry, but your parents have decided to separate. And they may get a divorce."

Jennifer moved away from Mom. "No, that can't happen! They wouldn't do that to me." She started to cry.

Mom tried to hug her again. "Of course they still love you. But this is an emotional time for them. They're trying to make it easier for you, Jennifer."

"No!" Jennifer cried. "I want to go home. Call my mother right now, and tell her I'm coming home."

"I know how hard this is for you, Jennifer," Mom said. "But try to understand. We'll call your mother. Maybe she can explain it better than I can."

"Why didn't my mother tell me herself?" she asked. "I want to talk to Mom and Dad right now."

"I'm sorry, Jennifer," David said. "We'll try to help you have a fun summer."

"A fun summer." Jennifer sobbed. "It's not

your parents who want to get rid of you. Laurie doesn't like me because I'm not a swimmer. I'm in everybody's way."

While she cried, I knew I had had it. I knew we were stuck with Miss Blonde New Yorker for three whole months.

Four

I think I'll always remember the day of the district invitational swim meet as one of the most embarrassing days of my whole life. I tried to run ahead so that nobody would know Jennifer was my cousin. But, of course, she had to sit on the bleachers with Mom and make a big deal of calling her "Aunt Liz."

It was cloudy and hot. Jennifer wore her slinky bathing suit and a gigantic hat. She said she brought the hat to keep the sun off her face. I think she wore it just to attract attention.

"Hey, that's a weird outfit your cousin's wearing," Susie whispered.

"Yeah," I said. "Now you know what I've been putting up with."

Susie nodded. We watched Jennifer zigzag

down the bleachers to where Bernie was sitting with some of the other swimmers. She practically threw herself at Bernie.

"Is there room for me to sit here?" Jennifer asked as she wiggled her way into a seat next to Bernie. She almost hit Bernie in the eye with that ridiculous hat.

Gail sat on the other side of Jennifer. Whatever Jennifer said, Gail laughed as if it were the funniest thing she'd ever heard.

I couldn't understand why she was so chummy with my cousin all of a sudden. Maybe it had something to do with David always being there, too.

"Let's go get a hot dog," Susie said. "We don't swim for two hours yet."

"Okay." Anything would be better than standing and watching my cousin perform, I thought.

Somehow Jennifer had torn herself away from Bernie long enough to hear Susie say "hot dog."

"Oh, would you bring me one, too, Laurie?" Jennifer asked. "A hot dog sounds absolutely scrumptious."

As Jennifer said the word "scrumptious," she batted her eyes at Bernie. He laughed nervously.

"I thought you didn't eat bread," I said loudly.

She gave me a cold look. "I do sometimes," she answered.

Susie and I took off for the refreshment stand.

"Mustard and relish," Jennifer called musically. Bernie laughed again.

"Yuck, what a flirt," I said.

"She's really something," Susie said.

After waiting in line for nearly half an hour, we took the hot dogs back and sat down to eat.

"Do you suppose I could have something to drink?" Jennifer asked as I took my first bite.

I gave her my I'll-kill-you look.

"I'll get some colas," Bernie said.

I stayed away from Jennifer the rest of the day. I didn't place in either one of the individual events. I had hoped for at least a sixth place ribbon to wave in front of Jennifer's face. She wouldn't know that the competition was much greater at a district invitational meet.

Eighteen teams were competing in this meet compared to two teams in a regular meet. That meant there were eighteen times as many eleven- and twelve-year-old girls who had better times than I did. It was depressing to think about it. My only chance for a ribbon now was to swim well in the relay.

Coach Bob was sitting in a lawn chair in the front row of the spectator section. I wormed my way through the crowd up to him.

"Hey, Bob." I tried to sound casual. "I'll get to swim in the relay today, won't I?"

"No, Laurie." Coach Bob studied his schedule. "I'm going to let Kathy Martin swim."

"Kathy Martin?" I was shocked. "But she's only ten."

"Yes, but we don't have a nine- and ten-year-old relay, and she's an excellent swimmer. With Kathy swimming for us in the next older category, our girls are sure to place," the coach said.

"But I've worked so hard, and I'm the right age."

"This is your first year," Coach Bob explained. "And it's your first district invitational meet. If you swim, the girls might not win a ribbon."

I could think of no more reasons to give him, so I zigzagged back through the crowd. Dark clouds rolled overhead. When it began to rain, all the parents ran inside with their programs over their heads. I felt like the weather, gloomy.

As I went in, I saw Jennifer coming in with Bernie holding an umbrella over her. Disgusting, I thought. They sat there all wrapped up in what *she* was saying.

Then the loudspeaker crackled. A voice announced that the rain had passed and the relays were starting.

Our girls came in fifth. Their ribbons were really cool. They were bright green with a big pleated ruffle. I wished in the worst way I could have won one.

David came in second in the eleven- and twelve-year-old boys' relay. When he came back from claiming his ribbon, I asked him if I could see it.

"Sure." He handed it to me.

It was bright red, smooth and glossy. It was nothing like our usual dual meet ribbons.

"It's beautiful. Congratulations, David."

"Thanks. I'm sorry you didn't get to swim," he said.

"Me, too." It was the first nice thing he'd said to me in days.

"Come on, we're going now," David said.

Walking together with David toward the parking lot made me feel good. David and I had always been a twosome before Jennifer had come to stay with us. Then I remembered I'd left my shirt in the gym.

"I forgot my shirt. I'll get it. Wait for me in the car."

As I ran, it began to rain again. I splashed through the puddles and got mud all over my legs. My shirt was right where I had left it. I grabbed it and ran back out into a downpour. Thunder roared, and lightning lit up the dark sky. The rain plastered my hair on my head, and water dripped off my nose. I pulled my towel up to cover my head. Finally I spotted the car, because Mom was blinking the headlights at me. I jumped in, soaking wet.

"What took you so long?" David asked.

"Lots of people were running in all directions." My teeth chattered as I spoke.

"You look like a drowned rat," Jennifer said.

"No, rats don't swim," David said. "She's a drowned otter."

Jennifer laughed. I looked at her with every blonde curl in place and not a drop of rain on her swimsuit. I looked at David who was grinning from ear to ear. Right then I hated Jennifer with all the energy I had left.

"At least I didn't spend all day making a

fool of myself over Bernie Wysowski," I said.

"Laurie!" Mom said.

"It's true, Mom. She did make a fool of herself and of me, too. All the kids were talking about it." I pouted, feeling steamy and uncomfortable.

"I notice you didn't win any ribbons," Jennifer said. "I guess you wasted the whole day trying to show what a big athlete you are."

"I'd rather be an athlete than boy-crazy," I said. "And I think eye shadow at your age is ridiculous."

"Well, that depends on your point of view," David said. He bent toward Jennifer's face with that idiot grin still on his face.

Jennifer smirked at David. "Laurie just doesn't understand our point of view, does she?"

That did it. "Understand?" I screamed. "I understand all right. I understand that your parents aren't just separated. They're getting divorced!"

"Laurie!" Mom said. "That will be enough."

I bit my quivering lip and stared out the window at the rain. Jennifer started to cry softly.

Then I did feel like a drowned rat. I hadn't meant to be that mean to Jennifer. I only wanted to fight back a little because she was being mean to me. It just slipped out about the divorce. I took a deep breath and decided I'd better keep my mouth shut. We rode without talking all the way home.

Five

"DAVID, please tell your cousin that I have picked up my half of the room. Ask her if she would please pick up her half," I said, even though Jennifer was sitting at my desk.

"Laurie says to ask you if you will please pick up *your* half of *her* room." David rolled his eyes at the ceiling.

"Tell your sister I will be happy to do it as soon as I finish filing my nails," Jennifer said.

"Jennifer says...," David began.

"I heard. Tell her I can't stand to be in this messy room any longer." I walked out with my nose in the air.

"Oh, brother," David said. "Why don't you tell her yourself?"

I wasn't speaking to Jennifer because of our

fight. Mom had suggested that I apologize and make up. I knew I should, but I just hadn't found the right moment. Actually, I thought Jennifer could do a little apologizing herself.

Then Dad called us into the living room and announced we were going out for dinner. I knew that would be a little awkward since Jennifer and I weren't speaking. But Dad looked so pleased with his idea I didn't say anything.

We went to Anderson's, my favorite restaurant. On the outside it looked like a huge sailing ship. Inside there were anchors and fishing nets all around, and the waiters wore sailor suits.

The restaurant was unusually busy. I was worried we wouldn't get a table by the big windows. Luckily some people were leaving, so we got a good table. I had a great view of the sunset on the lake.

"It's beautiful," Jennifer said.

"Just like you." David started clowning around again.

Jennifer giggled and tossed her blonde hair. I frowned at David. He was really beginning to bug me.

"Dad, may I have a quarter to play some music?" I asked when the waiter had finished taking our dinner order.

"Sure, go ahead." Dad handed me a quarter. I walked over to the jukebox and made a selection. As I slid back into my seat, I got instantly sick. Bernie Wysowski and his parents were standing by the door.

Oh, no, I thought. The only empty table was right next to ours. The three of them were walking straight toward us. I wanted to disappear. Or better still, I wanted to make Jennifer disappear.

"How are you, Art?" Dad stood to shake Mr. Wysowski's hand.

"Not bad. How are you doing, Carl?" Mr. Wysowski asked.

Mom and Mrs. Wysowski started talking, too. Bernie and Jennifer said "hi" and just stared at each other. It was disgusting.

The Wysowskis sat down about the same time the waiter brought our food. The funny thing was, I had been so hungry before. Now my appetite was completely gone. I pushed the mashed potatoes around on my plate.

"Laurie, I thought you were starving," Mom said.

"I lost my appetite," I told her.

Mom and Dad looked at each other.

The Wysowskis ordered from our waiter.

When he brought their salads, Jennifer called him over and ordered dessert. That meant we had to sit there longer. I was afraid to look at my cousin, I was so mad. It was like I knew what was going to happen—Bernie asked Jennifer to dance.

Since they were the only ones on the dance floor, everybody watched them. They danced all the new dances, not even noticing what a display they were making of themselves.

"David, why don't you dance with Laurie?" Dad suggested.

"No, I don't think so." I gave Dad a dirty look.

"Dance with my sister?" David put his hands at his throat and pretended he was strangling. "But I will dance with Jennifer." He wiggled his eyebrows and waved his pretend cigar in his Groucho Marx imitation.

The song ended, and the Wysowskis clapped for Bernie and Jennifer. Bernie went to put more money in the juke box.

David grabbed Jennifer's hand and spun her onto the floor. They stood there until the record started, and then they began to dance. David couldn't do all the fancy steps that Bernie did, so he shuffled his feet and swayed to the music. Jennifer smiled at him and danced in circles around him.

I was afraid to move. Half of me wanted Bernie to ask me to dance. The other half was terrified that he *would* ask me. I wasn't much better at dancing than David. I tried to look out the window, but it was dark by that time. My chair faced the dance floor, so there was nothing to do but watch.

When the dance was over, the adults clapped. Bernie claimed Jennifer for the next dance.

"Excuse me." I got up as fast as I could and raced to the restroom. I splashed cold water on my face. Then I dried my face with a paper towel and studied my reflection in the mirror. It's hopeless, I thought. Nobody will ever ask me to dance. Why should they? I don't even know how.

I returned to the table after I had wasted as much time as possible. Jennifer and Bernie were still wiggling at each other. The song ended, and another one started up. Jennifer and Bernie kept right on dancing.

"David," Dad said in a loud whisper. "Ask Laurie to dance." He pointed at me and winked at David.

I could feel myself turning fifty shades of red. Why did I feel like a charity case?

David stood up and bowed to me. "May I have this dance, please?"

"Oh, David, stop it," I hissed.

"Go on, Laurie, dance," Mom coaxed. "You'll have fun."

Reluctantly I got up and danced with my brother. I was so embarrassed. I could feel a million eyes staring at me. David and I sort of shuffled at each other. He didn't smile like he did when he danced with Jennifer. I guess he was embarrassed, too.

I tried to turn around in time to the music. David bumped into me and stepped on my foot, hard.

"Oh, I'm sorry," he whispered. "Did I hurt you?"

"No," I whispered back. But my foot did hurt. I looked over at Jennifer and Bernie smiling at each other. I wondered what it would be like to be dancing with Bernie instead of my brother.

"My, I sure am getting a workout," Jennifer said breathlessly when we sat down. She pushed her blonde hair out of her eyes and looked at me to make sure I was watching.

Finally Dad said, "It's been fun, but we'd better go. We all have to get up early tomorrow."

"Oh, no," David said, hamming it up. "I have to dance with Jennifer one more time."

Jennifer giggled hysterically. "There will be other dances, David."

"Yeah, it's time to go," I said. I smiled in relief. Then I had a comforting thought. Tomorrow is swim practice.

Six

I was not speaking to Jennifer now more than
ever. But it was difficult to avoid her all the
time. When David suggested that the three of
us walk over to the pool, I agreed against my
better judgment.

David and I wore flip flops, and we had our
suits on under our shorts—but not Jennifer.
She wore a fancy tennis dress and high-heeled
shoes. I bet she doesn't know the difference
between a tennis racket and a baseball bat, I
thought. All the way to the pool she
complained about walking and bragged about
how great the New York subways were. I've
been on the subway, and you get hot in there,
too.

I dived in the water as soon as I got there.
When I came up for air, who should I see

talking to David and Jennifer? Bernie, of course. That meant trouble.

"Want a cola?" David asked, as I joined them at the umbrella table.

"No, but I'll drink some of yours," I said. I grabbed David's cola and downed it in one gulp.

"Laurie, cut it out." David was on his feet trying to grab his drink from my hand. I giggled and turned my back avoiding his grasp. He made a lunge for my arm, and I took a step backward. He landed in the middle of the table, knocking Jennifer's cola into her lap.

"Oh, no," she exclaimed, jumping to her feet.

"I'm sorry." David started to wipe the front of Jennifer's short dress with his napkin. "Laurie, will you cut it out? Now see what you made me do?"

"Well, you shouldn't have started it," I retorted.

"Maybe we should wash her dress for her," Bernie teased.

"No, that's all right," Jennifer said.

"But your legs must be sticky." Bernie took a step toward Jennifer.

She backed up slowly. "No. No, really,

that's okay," Jennifer said.

Bernie grabbed Jennifer's shoulders with both hands and started dragging her toward the pool. "A nice swim would take care of everything," he said.

"No!" Jennifer shrieked. She wrestled out of his grip and ran toward the other end of the pool, still wearing those high-heeled shoes. I laughed.

Bernie laughed, too, and ran after her, catching up with her at the deep end. They giggled and struggled with each other, and then Bernie pushed Jennifer into the pool.

Jennifer surfaced, coughing and flailing her arms. "I can't swim," she gasped.

Bernie put his hands on his hips. "A likely story," he said.

Then I remembered what Jennifer had said her first day here. I ran over to Bernie. "She's telling you the truth. She really can't swim," I told him.

David and Bernie both dived into the pool, but Bernie reached Jennifer first. She clung tightly to him, but went under water a few more times before they finally got her out of the pool.

Jennifer lay on the concrete. A crowd had gathered around. "Move back," David yelled to the crowd. "Give her some air."

Bernie started to give her mouth-to-mouth resuscitation. Jennifer uttered a tiny gasp. Then her eyelids fluttered. She began coughing and sputtering. Tears streamed down her cheeks, and her face turned red. When she had quieted down, I put a towel under her head.

Someone had called the paramedics. When they got there, they said Jennifer was okay, just shaken. They praised David and Bernie for doing all the right things. The boys strutted around like they were heroes, even though it was Bernie who had pushed her into the pool in the first place.

The paramedics suggested that Jennifer take some swimming lessons. She wasn't too eager to go near water again. But David talked her into letting Coach Bob teach her how to swim.

* * * * *

The next day we took Jennifer over to meet Coach Bob. I had a feeling this wasn't going to be as easy as it sounded. At least Bernie wasn't around.

"So you're Laurie's cousin." Coach Bob

grinned. "I think I've seen you around." His voice sounded funny. Too bad yesterday was his day off, I thought. He could have seen Jennifer in action. Then he wouldn't be so impressed with her.

Jennifer batted her eyes at him. "I hope learning to swim isn't too hard."

"Naw, there's nothing to it." Coach Bob grinned at her again. "Can you put your face in the water?"

"I probably can, but I don't want to," Jennifer admitted.

"That's the first thing you have to do in order to learn how to swim," Coach Bob said seriously. "Sit down here on the step, and I'll show you."

They sat on the third step with the water lapping at their shoulders.

"Take a deep breath and hold it." The coach demonstrated by breathing in and sticking out his cheeks.

Jennifer followed instructions. I wished I'd had a camera.

"Now do the same thing, and put your face in the water," Coach Bob instructed.

Jennifer did what the coach said, but she had that almost-panicked look in her eyes as she brought her face out of the water.

"Great," Coach Bob said. "See? Swimming is going to be a snap."

"Okay, if you say so," Jennifer gasped.

I wasn't as convinced as Coach Bob was. Jennifer looked as if she might run away at any minute.

Coach Bob had Jennifer practice putting her face in the water a few more times. Then he got her to open her eyes under water. He held up two fingers and asked her how many she saw. I remembered that drill from when I was a little kid taking swimming lessons.

Coach Bob tried to teach Jennifer to float with her face in the water. She floated for about five seconds and then came up coughing and waving her arms like a drowning person.

"Don't breathe in. Blow bubbles, like this." The coach put his face in the water and demonstrated the technique.

Over and over Jennifer tried it. Every time she came up coughing. Her eyes began to get red from the chlorine, but she didn't complain.

"Let's practice kicking for a while," Coach Bob said. I could tell by the way he was frowning that he wasn't so impressed with Miss Gorgeous right now. He had Jennifer hang onto the side of the pool and do the freestyle kick.

"That's it," the coach said. "That's all for today. For homework I want you to practice holding your breath under water."

"Okay." Jennifer smiled at him. She looked relieved that the lesson was over.

Jennifer dragged herself out of the pool and collapsed on the chaise lounge.

"I'll help you with your breathing if you want," I said.

She looked at me. "Okay. Just let me rest for a while."

I wanted to say, See what hard work swimming is? But I was trying to be nice for a change, and I said nothing. Pretty soon Jennifer said she was ready, and we got into the pool. I dived in and came up after a long underwater swim. Jennifer was sitting on the steps waiting for me.

"Okay, just put your head under and blow bubbles the way Coach Bob showed you," I instructed.

Jennifer followed my suggestion. In two seconds she came up coughing.

"You have to remember to take a big breath first," I explained. "Then blow your air out gradually."

Jennifer took a big breath and blew the

bubbles. This time she didn't cough. She came up smiling.

"Try it again," I coached.

In went her face, and out she came coughing again. "I always forget and start to breathe," Jennifer said, exasperated.

"Try blowing only half of your air out," I suggested. "Then you won't be in such a hurry to breathe in again."

"Okay." Jennifer took a breath, put her face in the water, and blew the bubbles. She came up smiling. "It works," she said.

"Now, try floating and doing the same thing," I said.

Jennifer tried, but I guess there were too many things to remember. She panicked and came up too soon.

"Well, at least you're improving." I tried to be positive.

"Don't you think you've had enough for today?" David asked Jennifer from the side of the pool.

"The coach told her to practice," I said.

"So she practiced. Call it a day. She's tired." David smiled at Jennifer. She smiled back at him.

"Okay. I was only trying to help." The way David was sticking up for her, you'd think I was the bad guy. I got out of the pool and dried off.

"Thanks, Laurie, you were a big help," Jennifer called.

"You're welcome," I said.

From the chaise lounge I watched Jennifer and David talking. He knelt on the edge of the pool while she sat on the steps. I wondered what the big conversation was all about.

Seven

WE were swimming the last meet of the season against Pine Valley. Finally, I would get to swim in the relay again, because Susie was on vacation. In a way I wished the coach would let me swim breaststroke instead of freestyle. Then I wouldn't have to swim last.

I was really nervous when we lined up to swim. Gail, the backstroker, swam first. She finished even with her opponent. Melissa swam next with the butterfly. She got about a ten-yard lead on the Pine Valley girl. The crowd was cheering like crazy. Then came Allyson, swimming Susie's stroke, the breaststroke. My stomach was already doing flipturns. Allyson, our best swimmer, gained an even bigger lead. I was still nervous when it was my turn. I dived in, swimming my hardest. At every turn I could hear all the kids yelling, "Pull, pull."

But there was nothing to worry about. We won the medley relay by half a pool's length. The parents were all cheering and congratulating us.

The anticipation of claiming a blue ribbon is the best feeling in the whole world. The four of us marched up to the ribbon table together—but not right away. We didn't want to appear too eager.

Mrs. Fortis handed us the ribbons. "Nice swim, girls."

"Thanks," we said. I felt like screaming, *I won—I won!* and running around the pool, but I didn't. I went with the other girls to give our ribbons to our mothers.

"That was wonderful Laurie. You were great," Mom said. She was embarrassing me. She was trying to hug me even though I was dripping wet.

"Thanks." I didn't look at Jennifer, but I hoped she was watching me.

David won some blue ribbons, too. We kept Mom busy collecting them.

By the time the freestyle relay came around, we were positive we would win the meet. Since

Pine Valley was our big rival, everyone was in a great mood.

"If we win, let's throw all the parents in the pool after the meet," Allyson said.

"What do you mean, *if* we win?" Gail said with a chuckle.

"Yeah," Melissa said. "Fathers, too."

The word got around fast. We could hardly swim we were so excited. As we stood in line to swim the freestyle relay, I felt more confident. I guess winning is a feeling that's easy to get used to.

"Good luck, Laurie," Allyson said, patting me on the back.

"Thanks. You, too."

Allyson nodded at me and got up on the block. She was swimming second. Melissa climbed out of the pool.

"Nice swim," I said to Melissa.

"Thanks," she said with a big smile.

We cheered for Allyson when she came around for her turn. Then I got on the block. My dive was perfect—I couldn't believe it. Even my turns were pretty good. I heard the other girls cheering for me. It was the best sound in the whole world. Again we won the race by a big margin.

When Bernie's father said, "And the winner

is . . ." on the loudspeaker, the kids started cheering before he could announce the news. The coach waved his arms for us to be quiet.

"The winner is South Shore, 232, to Pine Valley, 168."

"Hurray!" A mass of grins and arms and legs rushed forward, picked up Coach Bob, and tossed him into the pool. The silly green hat he wore at the meets floated on top of the water. Everyone cheered.

"Mrs. Jones . . . get Mrs. Jones," yelled Bernie.

The mass of arms and legs melted over to Melissa's mother and threw her in. Suddenly the kids broke into small groups and headed for the nearest parent. Some of the adults stopped smiling and eased away from the pool to the parking lot. But some weren't quick enough.

"Mrs. Fortis, would you like to go for a swim?" Bernie asked.

"Definitely not," Mrs. Fortis said. But it didn't do any good. In she went.

Then they started dunking kids. "Get Laurie . . . get Laurie!" I heard someone say. The next thing I knew I was swimming in the deep end.

"Hi, Mom. Enjoying yourself?" I giggled.

"Very funny," Mom said.

"Yuck," Mrs. Fortis said, wringing out her tennis shoes as she held onto the side of the pool.

I think we would have gone on pushing everybody in all night if the parents hadn't demanded that we go home.

I scanned the pool for Jennifer. I spotted her sitting by herself at the far side. I dived into the pool and swam over to her.

"It's time to go," I said.

"Okay," she answered. She didn't look very happy.

"Don't you think it's great that we won the meet?"

"Yeah, I think it's great." She walked toward the car.

"You're jealous because you didn't get thrown in, right?" I ran alongside her. "Well, maybe I should just push you in, if that's what you want."

Jennifer stopped and looked at me. She wasn't mad, but somehow her look made me ashamed of what I'd said. She continued walking.

I ran over to get my towel and shirt. Big deal, I thought. So she doesn't like swimming. That's not my fault.

* * * * *

Jennifer was still timid the next day during her swimming lesson. She looked like she was about to cry.

"Jennifer, you're doing great," Coach Bob said. "Let's see how far you can swim today."

Jennifer pushed off from the side of the pool. She swam the freestyle perfectly until she had to take a breath. Then she came up coughing and waving her arms.

"Jennifer, it's not that hard," I said, giggling. "You have a mental block against taking a breath."

"Let's try again," Coach Bob told her.

"No. I'm not going to swim with my own cousin making fun of me." She climbed out of the water and ran to the locker room.

"What's wrong with her?" David asked, as he emerged from the pool.

"Oh, nothing. She got all excited because I laughed at how she swims."

"Give her a break," David said. "She's trying her hardest."

"I didn't mean to laugh *at* her—just at my joke. Besides, she's such a baby. She never wants to get her face wet."

"She's still learning. You've been awfully

hard on Jennifer this summer, Laurie. How would you like to have your parents getting a divorce, and have to spend the summer with a bratty cousin who picks on you all the time?"

"Well, at least she has you and Bernie flirting with her. She probably doesn't have time to notice what I do or say," I said.

"That's what really bothers you, isn't it? It's not Jennifer. It's just that you don't get all the attention you're used to."

"Oh, shut up, David. Who appointed you my shrink?" I got my towel and dried off.

"One more thing. I had a talk with Jennifer. She's had it with you and Ohio. She wants to go home."

"So, who's stopping her?"

"Think about it, Laurie. Do you want to be the one who drives her away?" David stormed off, no doubt looking for Miss Beauty Queen.

I hated it when David lectured me. I thought about what he said and decided he always did have a talent for stretching the truth.

Eight

"SWIM team picnic?" Jennifer asked. "What in the world do you do at a picnic? It sounds boring to me."

"Lots of things," I said. "They have paddle boats, swimming, volleyball, and a ton of food. You don't have to go if you don't want to."

"You'll have a good time, Jennifer," David said. "The lake is so beautiful that it's fun just to sit and look at it."

"New York City has so many activities that we don't ever amuse ourselves looking at lakes."

"So stay home." I slammed the door.

But Jennifer did go to the picnic. After lunch she and Bernie rented a paddle boat and went up the tree-shaded river that empties into the lake. I had an uneasy feeling about letting them out of my sight, but Gail was with me. We sat under a shade tree drinking lemonade. Melissa joined us.

"Who do you think will get the most valuable swimmer trophy in our age group?" Gail asked.

"Allyson's a cinch for 'most valuable,'" Melissa said.

"Oh, come on, Melissa," Gail said. "You think you'll get it, don't you?" Gail could be a brat sometimes.

"No, I don't. Do you?" Melissa wrinkled her nose.

"Who do you think will get 'most improved'?" I asked.

"That's a tough one," Gail said. "We all have improved our times."

"Laurie, didn't I see Bernie and your cousin go out in a paddle boat?" Melissa asked.

"I don't know," I said.

"I wonder what they could possibly be doing out there for so long?"

Susie came over and stretched out in front of us. She saved me from having to answer Melissa's nosy question.

"Laurie, did you know Bernie and your cousin are out on the lake in a paddle boat together?" Susie whispered.

Everybody laughed.

"What's so funny?" Susie asked.

"It's funny, because Melissa just asked Laurie the same thing," Gail said.

"Well, Laurie, what *do* you think they're doing out there all this time?" Melissa asked again.

"I don't know. Talking, I guess." I wished Melissa would be quiet.

"I know," Melissa said, "let's go for a walk in the woods and see if we can find them."

"That's a good idea," Gail said, jumping to her feet.

They were all the way down the path before I could say anything, so I didn't have any choice but to tag along.

Then Melissa called in a loud whisper, "Hey. Look what I found. Over here."

We all went running.

"It's Bernie and Jennifer. Look!"

Susie and Gail peered through a hole in the bushes. I pushed my way past them.

"Shhh," Melissa said.

There they were, sitting in the paddle boat under a willow tree, their arms around each other.

"I wonder what else they've been doing out there," Susie whispered.

The girls giggled quietly, straining and pushing against each other to get a view of the "real thing."

"I wonder how many times he's kissed her," Gail said, glancing at me.

As if on cue, their lips met in a long kiss.

I could feel my face getting hot. How could Jennifer do this to me in front of my friends?

"Look, they came up for air," Melissa said.

The girls held their hands over their mouths to keep from laughing out loud.

"Come on, let's go." I started down the path. "We shouldn't spy on them."

"Why not, Laurie?" Melissa blocked my way. "Do you know something about your cousin that we don't? After all, she is older than we are. She does come from the city and wears makeup and a bra and everything."

"I don't know what you're talking about," I said. "Get out of my way, please."

I hurried from the clearing to the main path. Tears stung my eyes as I saw my friends pull the bushes apart for the latest glimpse of the "love boat."

"There you are, Laurie," Mrs. Fortis said. "We've been looking for you. Where are the others?" she asked.

I stared at her for a minute. I didn't want

her peeking through the shrubs at Bernie and Jennifer. "Well, I . . . uh . . . I don't know," I stammered. "I lost them myself."

"Oh, dear." Mrs. Fortis looked annoyed. She went down the path calling, "Susie. Gail. Melissa. Time to go."

The girls came out of the woods still giggling.

"What seems to be so funny?" Mrs. Fortis asked.

Her question only made them laugh harder. I felt my face getting hot again. I concentrated on hating Jennifer so I wouldn't cry.

"Hurry, it's starting to rain," Mrs. Wheeler called.

Everybody grabbed their stuff from the picnic tables and ran to the cars. Bernie and Jennifer were the last to get in. Jennifer's eyes were shining.

When we got home, Mom wasn't there. David lay down on the couch in front of the TV.

"Want to play cards, Laurie?" Jennifer asked.

"Don't try to butter me up. It's too late now," I said.

"What are you talking about?" Jennifer asked. She looked surprised.

"You go to my swim team picnic and embarrass me in front of my friends. And then you pretend nothing has happened and say, 'Want to play cards?' " I walked around swinging my hips the way she did.

Her mouth fell open.

"Don't give me that injured look," I yelled. "I'm tired of you getting your own way with that poor-little-me act."

"What did I do to upset your majesty this time?" Jennifer was crying.

"You know darn well what you did," I said. "You went out in that paddle boat with Bernie Wysowski and made out so that all my friends could laugh at me for having that kind of cousin."

"Don't flatter yourself, you spoiled little brat." Jennifer stood in front of me with her hands on her hips. "I wouldn't purposely try to make your friends think anything, because I don't care what they think. And Bernie and I weren't making out, we were just talking.

"Believe it or not, Laurie, Bernie listens to my problems. He cares how I feel about my parents' divorce, which is more than I can say for you."

"You sure picked a great place to have that nice little talk. And you were too kissing. I saw you," I said. "Now, you're the laughing stock of the swim team."

"That's all I've heard all summer—swim team, swim team. You don't want me here. My parents don't want me. Nobody wants me," Jennifer sobbed.

"Gosh, Laurie, don't you know when to stop?" David handed Jennifer a tissue. "Let up on her," he said.

"Shut up and mind your own business," I snarled.

"All you do is make it harder for me, Laurie," Jennifer said between sobs.

"But you make it hard for *me*," I said. "You don't try to fit in at all."

"Just leave me alone. I don't want to be a bother to anybody." Jennifer ran crying to my room.

"Was all that really necessary?" David glared at me.

"Be quiet. I don't need your advice," I said.

"You're right. You need more than advice. You need something to straighten out your head."

I tried to ignore him, but I was mad and hurt at the same time. Just once I'd like him to see my side of the argument for a change.

Nine

"DAVID, have you seen Jennifer?" I asked, standing in the door of his room. I had just finished getting ready. Dad was taking us to the movies.

"No, I haven't seen her since lunch," David said, buttoning his gray shirt.

"That's funny. It takes her longer to get ready than it does me."

Dad appeared at the door. "Everybody ready? The bus leaves in five minutes. Where's Jennifer?"

"I was going to ask you the same question," I said.

We searched the house and discovered that Jennifer was nowhere to be found. Mom sent David over to Bernie's house to see if she was there. Mom called the neighbors. I said

I'd check at Gail's.

I rode down to Gail's on my bike, secretly mad at Jennifer for making me get sweaty after I had showered. She wasn't there. On the way home I even checked the garage and the backyard.

"Any luck?" Dad asked.

"Negative," I said.

"Bernie hasn't seen her since yesterday," David said.

"We'll wait a while," Dad said. "Maybe she decided to walk to the store."

"She has been awfully quiet lately," Mom said.

We sat in the living room, waiting for something to happen. Mom kept talking on the phone. I looked at David, but he stared at the floor. I hoped he wasn't going to blab about yesterday's fight.

After a while I decided to check my room for clues. It looked the same as always—crowded. I opened the closet. "Her clothes are gone!" I yelled.

"What did you say?" Mom called. Dad, Mom, and David all came into my room.

"Jennifer's gone!" I said. "She's taken her clothes." I pointed to Jennifer's half of my closet. It was completely empty.

"David, go out on your bike and look for her," Mom said.

"There's only a half hour left before the movie starts," I wailed. "Darn her. She ruins everything."

"If you hadn't had that fight with her yesterday, this never would have happened," David said as he left the room.

"Shut up, David," I called after him.

"What fight?" Dad asked.

"Oh, nothing."

"Laurie, what fight?" Mom asked.

Before I knew it, I was telling them the whole story about the picnic, the paddle boat, and the fight. A lump rose in my throat, and my stomach hurt again.

"I see," Dad said, sitting down on my bed.

"But I didn't mean to make her think I hated her," I said. "I just get so mad at her sometimes."

"I've called all the neighbors. No one has seen her. You don't suppose she would run away, do you, Carl?" Mom asked.

"We'll find her," Dad said. "Come on, Liz."

Mom and Dad went back to the telephone. I sat there trying to get my knees to stop shaking.

It's funny how things work out sometimes, I

thought. Jennifer bugged me all summer, so I let her have it. Now because of that she was missing, and I felt terrible. What if something bad happened to her? It's really rotten when there's nobody to blame but yourself.

When David came back, he was all excited. "I figured out where she is—I mean, where she's going."

"What do you mean?" Dad asked.

"She's on her way to New York," David said. "She told me a few days ago that she didn't know how much longer she could take staying here." David looked at me with reproach.

"How would she get there?" Mom asked. "She doesn't have much money."

"I hope she wouldn't think of hitchhiking," Dad said.

"Oh, Carl, do you think we should call the police?" Mom asked.

"There's only one direction she would go—east," Dad said. "Let's go out to Highway 23 and see if we can spot her. If we can't, we'll call the police."

We left David home in case Jennifer called. As we approached the highway, I sat forward on the seat looking for Jennifer. We rode a few blocks and then drove back the other way.

"We're wasting time," Mom said.

Dad kept circling the area where he thought she might be. I closed my eyes tight and prayed that Jennifer was all right. I thought about the horror stories you hear about hitchhiking.

Finally, Dad said, "I guess you're right, Liz."

When we got home, we silently watched Dad call the police.

In a very short time, two officers with badges and guns arrived. We gave them a description and a photograph of Jennifer.

"You say the last time she was seen was about lunchtime today?" the one called Officer Morgan asked.

"That's right," Dad said. "We think she might be trying to hitchhike to New York."

"Have you called her family?" Officer Morgan asked.

"No, but we will," Mom said.

"Do you remember what she was wearing?" the other policeman asked.

"I think she had on a pink shirt and shorts," I said. "She must have a suitcase with her, because she took all her clothes. Her suitcases are light blue."

The officer wrote down everything we said.

"Do you think you can find her?" Mom asked anxiously.

"We'll do our very best, ma'am," the officer said. "A high percentage of runaways are found. Working out their problems after they come back home seems to be the difficult part."

"She can't have gone very far." Dad sounded scared. I don't remember my dad ever sounding afraid before.

"If she calls, remember to call us right away. The number's on this card," the officer said as he and his partner were leaving. Dad stood frowning at the card.

The policemen were no help, I thought. I guess I had expected them to bring Jennifer back immediately. I felt like punching something, I was so disappointed. But I knew that wouldn't do any good. Getting angry wouldn't bring Jennifer back. Getting angry was the cause of this situation in the first place.

"We'd better call Karen," Mom said, her voice shaky. Mom dialed the phone and talked to Aunt Karen until she started to cry. Then Dad took over the phone.

"We're sorry we had to worry you," Dad apologized. "But we had to call in case she phones you," Dad went on.

I looked at David for comfort, but he sat with his hands in his pockets, avoiding my eyes.

"Don't worry, the police will locate her soon," Dad said, reassuringly. "Let us know immediately if you hear from her." He hung up.

Then we just sat and waited for the telephone to ring.

* * * * *

I woke up the next morning, and I still had my clothes on. I didn't remember going to bed. I went out to the living room and found Mom and Dad waiting by the telephone. David was staring at the television set.

I sat down and started staring at the TV, too. But I got tired of looking at the set and not seeing the picture. When the phone finally rang, everyone jumped.

Dad answered it. "They've found her," he said. "She's at the police station now. She's all right."

All the way to the police station I felt such relief. I was sure I could run alongside the car and not get tired. Even David grinned the whole time.

The clerk at the front desk told us where to go to find Jennifer. She was sitting on a chair in a room full of desks. She looked tired and lost, and her blonde hair was pretty scraggly. The officer cornered Dad and Mom to sign some papers, so David and I got to my cousin first.

"Jennifer, where were you?" I blurted out.

"I'm sorry I ran away," she said in a very low voice. "I thought I could hitchhike home easily. This old couple picked me up and told me they were going to New York. But they only took me as far as their farm. Then they called the police while I slept."

"I'm sorry I said those mean things to you," I said. "I guess I let my friends tease me until I got really mad."

Jennifer started to cry. "Nobody wanted me around—not you, not my parents, not anybody."

"That's not true," I said. "I want you. We all want you. I'm sorry I've been such a brat all summer. You can stay here and go to school with me if you want."

"Why should I? You don't like me. Nobody cares about me." Fresh tears streamed down her face.

"That's not true. I care about you. I guess I

didn't realize that until you ran away."

Jennifer looked at me oddly for a second, as if she wasn't sure she believed me.

Dad, Mom and Officer Morgan came over to us. "Running away from your problems doesn't solve anything," the officer said. "And it could get you in a lot of trouble.

"Yes, sir," Jennifer said. Mom gave Jennifer a hug, and Dad patted her shoulder.

"I'm so glad you're all right," Mom said to Jennifer. Then she added, "Honey, if things are that bad, we need to sit down and talk about the problems."

Jennifer looked right at me. "I think we have our problems worked out already," she said in a firm voice.

The dam burst and the tears started flowing. I couldn't stop them. "I'm so glad we found you," I said.

"What are we doing standing here?" David asked. "We could be home eating breakfast."

Jennifer laughed. David put his arm around her and winked at me. Dad put one arm around me and one arm around Mom. We all walked to the car together.

Ten

THE swim team banquet was planned for the Friday after Jennifer had tried to run away. Now that we had her back, I started to get excited about the banquet. I had begun to realize that the banquet wouldn't have meant as much without Jennifer. I had really won those ribbons to impress her. All summer I had been swimming for Jennifer. It was really weird, but that's the way it was.

I asked Jennifer to go shopping with me to find a dress for the banquet. I was a little nervous about another shopping trip with Miss World's Greatest Shopper. After all, I did remember the time she tried on forty million swimsuits. But this trip turned out better than I had hoped.

"What kind of dress do you want, Laurie?"

Jennifer asked as she browsed through the racks. Mom had dropped us off at the mall with the idea of picking us up in three hours. I figured that was all I could take of shopping.

"I don't really know. That's my problem," I confessed. "I don't want ruffles, but I don't want something too old for me either."

"The thing to do is just start trying on dresses," Jennifer advised. "Sooner or later, if you try enough of them on, you'll find something you like."

"Okay," I said. I could have guessed she'd say that.

Jennifer began selecting dresses and putting them over her arm. I was a little worried because I didn't even like half of the ones she was picking out.

"What do you think of this one?" I asked, holding up a yellow dress.

Jennifer looked at the dress and then at me. "It's not your color," she said. "Yellow looks better on blondes."

I bit my lip. No matter how chummy Jennifer and I got, there would always be parts of her personality that bugged me. I guess that was to be expected. Nobody was perfect.

It seemed to take forever to try on all the

dresses. The one I liked the best was one Jennifer had picked out, of course.

"It looks really nice on you, Laurie," Jennifer said, nodding her approval.

"I like it, too," I said. It was a plain, light blue knit dress. I could tell from the wistful look on Jennifer's face that she really did like it.

"What are you going to wear to the banquet?" I asked Jennifer when we were paying for my dress.

"My pink dress with the spaghetti straps," she said.

"Oh," I said. I had seen some pink ribbon bows on combs that would be just perfect for Jennifer's hair. And she had said she was going to wear her hair up, too.

Jennifer wandered over to the sportswear department. I had just enough time to pick up the combs and slip them to the saleslady. I pointed to Jennifer, and the lady nodded, smiling. She rang up the bows, and I gave her the money.

When we got home and were showing my dress to Mom, I gave Jennifer the pink bows.

"Oh, Laurie, they're beautiful," Jennifer said, giving me a hug. "You remembered I said I was going to wear my hair up."

"Now we both have something new to wear to the banquet," I said.

* * * * *

Finally, the night of the banquet arrived. I thought it would never get here. Jennifer helped me curl my hair. It didn't want to stay curled though. Jennifer's hair looked really great with the pink bows holding up all her blonde curls.

When we got to the banquet, we ran into Susie Wheeler and her parents. We decided to sit together. Gail and her parents were sitting at our table, too. All the kids looked so different dressed up. I was used to seeing them wet.

For dinner we had steak and baked potatoes. It was good, but I couldn't eat very much. Mom gave me a hug and whispered, "I understand why you can't eat. We'll ask for a doggie bag, and you can eat it later."

"Okay." I smiled at her.

After the dinner, the coach and some of the parents gave speeches. Finally, Coach Bob got around to presenting the trophies. Of course, he had to give speeches about each kid who won the eight-and-under trophies. Then he talked about the nine- and ten-year-olds. Finally, he got to the eleven- and twelve-year-old girls.

Jennifer looked at me. "I hope you get a trophy," she whispered.

"Thanks," I said.

"The most valuable swimmer is Allyson Bradley," Coach Bob said.

During the applause, Gail looked at me and said, "I told you so."

"Yeah," I said.

Allyson smiled as she accepted her trophy and stood by the others to be photographed. We clapped again.

"The next girl worked harder than anyone on the team," the coach said. "The most improved swimmer trophy goes to Laurie Mathews."

I stood up and walked to the platform. As Coach Bob said, "Congratulations," I realized I had really won a trophy . . . the trophy I had wanted to win. Everybody clapped. I stood with the others until they finished taking our pictures. When all the awards had been given out, we went back to our seats.

"Nice going, Sis." David grinned at me.

"Thanks." I grinned back.

"Congratulations, Laurie," Mom said,

hugging me. Dad gave me a big hug, too.

"I knew you'd win," Jennifer said, smiling.

"Thanks," I said.

Susie came over. "Let me see your trophy, Laurie," she said. I handed it to her. "It's really neat," she said, wistfully.

"Thanks." I knew I was grinning like an idiot, but I was too happy to care. Everybody kept congratulating me. I loved every minute of it.

* * * * *

When we got home, the telephone rang. "Jennifer, it's for you," Mom said.

"Me?" Jennifer said. "Who'd be calling me?"

"It's your mother, honey." Mom motioned for us to go into the other room.

Dad found a place on the bookcase for my trophy and the medal David had won.

Jennifer came in with a smile on her face. "Mom has already registered me for school," she said. "She's flying out tomorrow to take me back with her."

"What else did she say?" Mom asked.

"Oh, not much. She mostly talked about our new apartment and my new room. I guess that means I'll be going back to New York City for school after all." She looked at me.

"We'll miss you, Jennifer," I said.

"I'll miss you, too," she said. "I'm sorry I scared everybody so badly."

"Maybe you can come and stay with us next summer," David suggested.

"I'd like that."

"So would Bernie Wysowski," I said.

About the Author

BONNIE TOWNE lives with her husband and her two teenage children in St. Petersburg, Florida. *Why Doesn't She Go Home!* was Ms. Towne's first book. It was inspired by the activities of her own children, who were both on a swim team.

Ms. Towne is a writer and teacher of creative writing. Many of the ideas for her book *Hollywood Jr. High* came from the students of her seventh grade class. Vanessa Schranm

When she is not writing or teaching, Ms. Towne likes to swim, read, and walk on the beach. It was her beach walking on Sanibel Island that provided the setting for her book *A Summer To Remember*.